D0475404

POKÉMON

Trainer's Mini Exploration Guide to Sinnoh

POKéMON™

Trainer's Mini Exploration Guide to Sinnoh

INSIGHT
EDITIONS

San Rafael · Los Angeles · London

CONTENTS

Welcome to Sinnoh   6

Turtwig   8

Grotle   12

Torterra   14

Chimchar   16

Monferno   18

Infernape   22

Piplup   24

Prinplup   28

Empoleon   30

Riolu   32

Lucario   36

Combee   38

Vespiquen   42

Chatot   46

Croagunk   50

Toxicroak   54

Shellos and Gastrodon   56

Drifloon	58
Drifblim	62
Gible	64
Gabite	68
Garchomp	70
Uxie, Mesprit, and Azelf	72
Dialga and Palkia	76
Heatran	84
Regigigas	88
Giratina	92
Phione	94
Manaphy	98
Cresselia and Darkrai	100
Shaymin	104
Arceus	108

Welcome to Sinnoh!

Sinnoh is a region **steeped in history**. From the sprawling Underground to the top of Mt. Coronet, there are countless relics of the past to be found—as well as 107 new Pokémon to help you along the way! Whether you're seeking out completely new friends or maybe searching for a new Evolution for a longtime companion of yours, this guide will help you get started on your journey through Sinnoh!

TURTWIG #387

The shell on Turtwig's back is made of hardened soil, but photosynthesis occurs all across the rest of its body while it's in the sun, allowing Turtwig to **produce oxygen**! Much like a plant, though, the leaf on Turtwig's head wilts if it gets thirsty.

Ash's Turtwig had a habit of latching onto him as a show of affection, but it **doesn't bite him too hard**—hopefully.

"When Turtwig Bites you, it's a sign that Turtwig really likes you!"
—Clara

"When Turtwig evolves into Grotle, its body gets ten times heavier, and all in a very short time!"
—Brock

GROTLE #388

Now that Grotle has evolved, its soil shell is big enough for plants to grow—and it always knows where the **purest water** can be found to keep them healthy. As it travels to these water sources, it carries other Pokémon on its back.

TORTERRA #389

With a cluster of boulders and a sprawling tree on its back, it's no wonder that Torterra is called a Continent Pokémon! It's **so large**, in fact, that small Pokémon sometimes make their homes on its shell. Ancient people once believed that a giant Torterra lived under the ground!

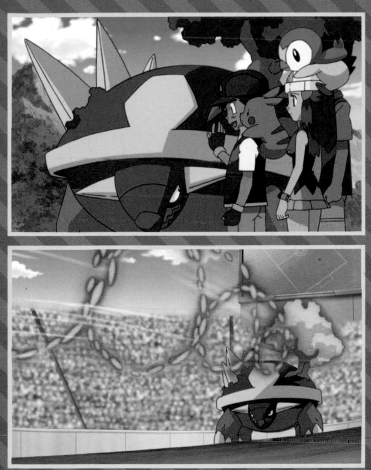

CHIMCHAR #390

Chimchar's fire is **fueled by a gas** it produces inside its stomach that can't be put out even by rain! But a sick or weakened Chimchar will have only a flickering flame that indicates it is unwell.

MONFERNO #391

With **incredible agility**, Monferno can use walls and ceilings to aid it in launching aerial attacks on its foes. Though it may sometimes use its tail as a weapon, it has many other options for attack, and can instead **burn** the flame on its tail intensely to keep foes at bay!

When sustaining major damage, Ash's Monferno would activate Blaze, which powers up its Fire-type attacks. But as much as it helps, Blaze also leaves Monferno in a **rage**, and it struggles to see reason.

However, with Ash's help, Monferno was able to overcome the rage of Blaze—and that experience was just what it needed to finally **evolve into Infernape**!

INFERNAPE #392

Infernape is as **fiery** as the crown of flames on its head. With a quickness to its movements that is nearly unmatched, it tosses enemies around with incredible agility and engages in combat using a unique fighting style that involves all its limbs.

PIPLUP #393

Piplup is a **very proud** Pokémon, which makes bonding with a Trainer difficult. It hates to accept food from people and doesn't like being taken care of. This pride can also get in the way of its Trainer's orders, and sometimes it **just won't listen**!

Stubborn to a fault, a Piplup refused to eat food Dawn offered when they first met, even though it was really hungry.

It warmed up to her quickly, though! After Dawn encouraged Piplup to leave her behind and escape the Ariados on its own, Piplup defended Dawn with Bide, taking the hits and unleashing a **powerful attack** in return!

"Prinplup in particular aren't thrilled being with others."
—Brock

PRINPLUP #394

Since each Prinplup believes it's the most important one, it's no wonder that Prinplup tend to live **solitary lives**. They live alone, but they can definitely take care of themselves—their wings deliver powerful blows that can snap trees!

EMPOLEON #395

Empoleon can swim as fast as a jet boat and is capable of slicing right through any ice in its way with the sharp edges of its wings! The horns that extend from its beak are a **sign of its power**, and in groups of Empoleon, the individual with the largest horns is the leader.

RIOLU #447

Full of **boundless energy**, Riolu has enough stamina to run all night long! This makes taking it for walks particularly difficult. Riolu can use waves called aura to tell how people are feeling and to determine the state of the environment around it!

Even while it was still in an Egg, Ash's Riolu was able to sense the aura in the surrounding area, **feeling the energy** of Ash's battle and calling out to him!

When it hatched, Riolu immediately ran off into the forest to try and find that same **aura** it had felt when Ash was battling.

LUCARIO #448

Lucario has grown capable of controlling auras, using the waves to take down foes and even destroy giant rocks! But it won't lend this strength to just anybody—Lucario **can tell what people are thinking** and only trusts Trainers with justice in their hearts.

COMBEE #415

The members of a Combee trio are **inseparable**, spending all their time together. Despite their varying tastes in nectar, they spend all day from sunrise to sundown gathering it for their swarm and Vespiquen!

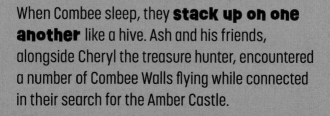

When Combee sleep, they **stack up on one another** like a hive. Ash and his friends, alongside Cheryl the treasure hunter, encountered a number of Combee Walls flying while connected in their search for the Amber Castle.

Combee and giant Combee Walls protected the **Amber Castle**, and the Vespiquen that lived inside!

VESPIQUEN #416

The more **pheromones** Vespiquen gives off, the larger the swarm of Combee attendants this Pokémon has. When threatened, Vespiquen skillfully commands its grubs, who are more than willing to risk their lives in battle to defend it.

At the heart of the Amber Castle, Ash, Dawn, Brock, and Cheryl found Vespiquen, who was angry at their intrusion and sought to drive them out. However, after seeing their efforts to keep the Amber Castle from falling apart, Vespiquen chose to entrust them with some **Enchanted Honey**!

CHATOT #441

Chatot has a **knack for mimicry**. It makes other Pokémon think it's one of them by copying their cries so that it won't get attacked, and it can even mimic human speech! If a group of them get together, they'll all end up learning the same phrase.

Ash and his friends met Ada and her partner, Chatot, while traveling in the Hoenn region. Chatot and Ada were a **comedy duo**, with Chatot using its mimicry abilities to serve as one half of the act. Chatot frequently flew off to entertain the children at a local hospital with its copycat skills!

CROAGUNK #453

Croagunk attempts to catch its opponents off-guard by making frightening noises with the sacs on its cheeks. If they flinch, it immediately retaliates with a **poisonous** jab.

However, Croagunk's poison isn't just for attacking—when **diluted**, it can be used as a **medicine**!

In Pastoria City, Ash and his friends learned that Croagunk are considered the guardians of the Great Marsh and are treated with immense respect. Every household raises a Croagunk, and they are so beloved that there's even an entire **festival** dedicated to them every year!

"Toxicroak, time for fun!"
—Saturn

TOXICROAK #454

When battling a Toxicroak, watch out for its **poisonous claws**! Just a scratch is all that's needed to knock out an opponent, and when its foes go down, it lets out a booming victory croak. They may not look like it, but Toxicroak and Seismitoad are actually related species!

SHELLOS #422

GASTRODON #423

Ash and his friends met a pink Shellos early on in their adventures—and were surprised to later discover a group of Shellos that were not only blue, but also looked a little different. They learned that when Mt. Coronet was first starting to form, it **split the populations** of Shellos and its evolved form, Gastrodon.

Each side adapted to its habitat, becoming the two colors known today—**pink on the western side of Sinnoh, and blue on the eastern side!**

DRIFLOON #425

In **search of company**, Drifloon approaches children—however, if they play too roughly, it quickly runs away! During humid seasons, it is common to see Drifloon appear in great numbers.

Drifloon can be **really strong**: Nurse Joy's daughter, Marnie, used three of them to take her dad's lunch to him. All she had to do was hold on and let them carry her off into the sky!

DRIFBLIM #426

Drifblim is said by some to be a **collection of souls** that are burdened by their regrets. Drifting silently through the night, it grabs people and Pokémon and carries them off. No one knows where it takes them—except for Drifblim, that is.

**"Pikachu's Thunderbolt is
too strong to take!"**
—Zoey

**"But a Blimp Pokémon like Drifblim can
dodge moves like that so easily that it
almost seems like it's controlling them!"**
—Brock

GIBLE #443

In order to stay warm no matter the weather, Gible makes its home in narrow holes in cave walls that are **heated** by geothermal activity.

Attacking anything that moves, Gible drags its catches back into its small lair, but it often bites off more than it can chew—literally! Gible's mouth may be big, but its stomach is actually rather small.

Ash's Gible **struggled** for a long time trying to learn Draco Meteor—instead of a shower of meteors, it often summoned just a single meteor that would land on Dawn's Piplup!

In addition, Ash's Gible liked to **bite anything** it could, including Ash's head and an opposing Trainer's Shuckle!

GABITE #444

Gabite uses **ultrasonic waves** to find its way around dark caves. The caves this Pokémon nests in have jewels buried in the depths, but the moment you set foot in one of these caves, you're liable to be met by the claws and fangs of a very angry Gabite!

GARCHOMP #445

Garchomp flies at **incredible speeds**. When it leaves its blazing volcano home to hunt, it flies as fast as a jet plane and brings back as much prey as it can carry—all before its body even has a chance to completely cool!

LEGENDARY

UXIE #480

MESPRIT #481

AZELF #482

These **three Legendary Pokémon** are said
to have granted various attributes to humans before
settling at the bottoms of three lakes across Sinnoh
to observe the world. In their adventures through the
region, Ash and his friends each happened to spot one
of these **rare** Pokémon.

Uxie appeared before Brock at **Lake Acuity**, Dawn saw Mesprit at **Lake Verity**, and Ash spotted Azelf at **Lake Valor**!

When Azelf was **attacked** and captured by Team Galactic, its two counterparts arrived to try and help, but Uxie and Mesprit ended up **captured** as well.

However, they were able to reach out to Ash and his friends for help, even teleporting the trio and their Pokémon right into the Team Galactic base!

A Legendary Pokémon, Dialga is not only said to have the power to **control time**, but also is believed that time only started when Dialga was born. In Sinnoh mythos, it is considered an ancient deity.

DIALGA #483

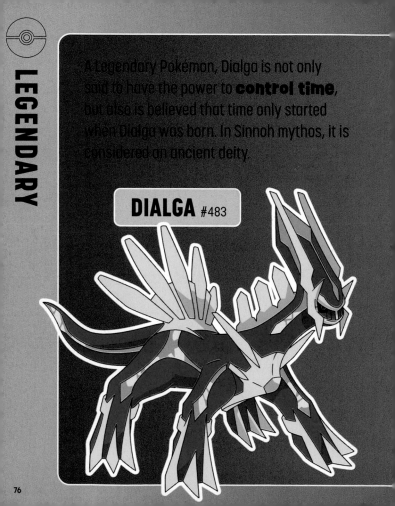

PALKIA #484

Also considered a deity in the Sinnoh region, Palkia is said to hold **dominion over space**. It does not live in the same dimension as us, instead making its home in a gap of the spatial dimension that exists as a parallel to ours.

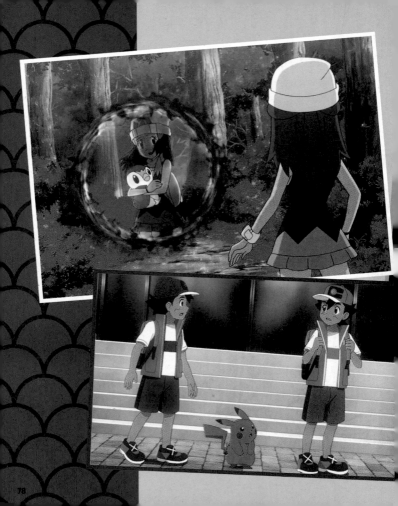

When Team Rocket forced Palkia and Dialga to fight, Palkia opened portals to other worlds—not just Ash and his friends' home world, but also an **alternate world** that mirrored theirs, where they met themselves!

During its forced battle with Palkia, Dialga's control over time went haywire, **reversing the flow of time**. With time going backward, Pokémon started forgetting moves, and even devolving and turning back into Eggs! In the alternate world, this had happened to Dawn's Piplup and Ash's Pikachu. They missed them so much!

Ash, Dawn, Goh, Chloe, and their alternate-world selves went to the dimension where Palkia and Dialga were being forced to fight. Before they could break their chains, Dialga's power turned all their Pokémon into Eggs—and all of them into **young children**!

They embraced their love of Pokémon and used Palkia's portals, together with people around the world, to call upon a Mythical Pokémon.

Sensing the world's **love** for Pokémon, Arceus appeared and freed them, allowing Palkia and Dialga to restore both worlds to normal and send everyone home!

HEATRAN #485

Heatran lives deep within volcanic caves, crawling on ceilings and walls with its cross-shaped feet. The blood that runs through Heatran's body is said to **boil like magma**!

A Pokémon Ranger named Ben sought out Heatran so he could take the Pokémon to the National Park. He found it in a magma-filled cavern, where Heatran could use Flash Fire to **absorb energy** from the heat of the magma!

"Heatran always live near volcanoes, so it stands to reason that it would be somewhere where the ground feels warm to the touch!"
—Ben

REGIGIGAS #486

Existing in legends as a being that towed the continents with ropes, Regigigas is truly a **Colossal** Pokémon. It's believed to have created Regice, Regirock, and Registeel in its image from elements of the world itself.

Protected by three pillars of rock, ice, and steel, Regigigas slumbered deep within Snowpoint Temple. But Pokémon Hunter J gave it a rude awakening, and it became seriously **enraged**, destroying the temple it called home!

As a result of the **kindness and sacrifice** shown by Brandon and his Pokémon, Regigigas calmed down from its raging fury and returned to slumber. Brandon then swore to rebuild the temple and have his own Regirock, Regice, and Registeel become the three guardian pillars to protect Regigigas.

GIRATINA #487

For violent acts in ages long past, Giratina has been **banished** to a world on the reverse side of ours. In this realm, where common knowledge is distorted, Giratina gazes silently upon the old world, its former home.

PHIONE #489

When the water grows warm, Phione drifts gently on the ocean currents in packs. But no matter how far they roam, they always **return home**, to the place where they were born.

Phione's migration is so consistent that Chocovine Town has a festival each year when the Pokémon pass through the area. There's even a superstition that anyone who sees Phione is sure to have **good luck**!

"There's an old saying in Chocovine Town: 'Good luck smiles down on those who spot the Phione.'"
—resident

One Phione became so **enamored** with Dawn's Buneary that it wanted to battle for the chance to go on a date!

MANAPHY #490

From the very beginning of its life, Manaphy has a **wondrous power** that allows it to bond with any kind of Pokémon there is!

LEGENDARY

CRESSELIA #488

DARKRAI #491

While Ash and Goh were investigating an outbreak of **nightmares** leaving people sleepless and irritable, signaling the possible appearance of Darkrai, Chloe met Dawn and the two of them encountered an injured Cresselia.

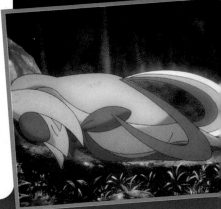

Though they originally believed the two Legendary Pokémon were enemies and Darkrai had hurt Cresselia, it turned out to be the **opposite**—when Cresselia fled Fullmoon Island after being attacked by Team Rocket, Darkrai followed to help its injured friend make its way back home!

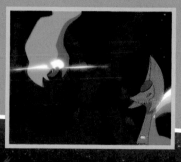

104

SHAYMIN #492

Shaymin can turn a ruined land into a beautiful field of flowers by **dissolving toxins** in the air. Gracidea blooms grant it the power of flight, and it delivers messages in the form of feelings of gratitude!

The gratitude Mallow and her mother expressed for each other caused many Gracidea flowers to **bloom**—and among the flowers was a Shaymin, which chose to stay with Mallow until the next Gracidea season.

After sniffing a bouquet of Gracidea flowers, Mallow's friend Shaymin changed into its **Sky Forme** and flew off with a bunch of its friends!

ARCEUS #493

Arceus is said to have emerged from an Egg before the universe existed. A pillar of **ancient mythology**, it is said to have shaped all there is upon the world.

When Palkia and Dialga's battle threatened multiple worlds and their inhabitants, Ash and his friends—as well as their alternate selves—called out to Arceus to help them. Arceus intervened, breaking the power of the Red Chain to **free** the two Legendary Pokémon from their conflict!

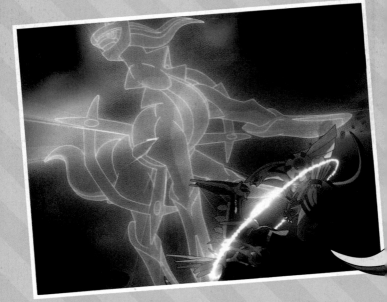

INSIGHT EDITIONS

PO Box 3088
San Rafael, CA 94912
www.insighteditions.com

Find us on Facebook: www.facebook.com/InsightEditions
Follow us on Twitter: @insighteditions

ISBN: 978-1-64722-985-6

Text by Kay Austin

Publisher: Raoul Goff
VP, Co-Publisher: Vanessa Lopez
VP, Creative: Chrissy Kwasnik
VP, Manufacturing: Alix Nicholaeff
VP, Group Managing Editor: Vicki Jaeger
Publishing Director: Mike Degler
Designer: Leah Bloise Lauer

Associate Editor: Sadie Lowry
Editorial Assistant: Alex Figueiredo
Managing Editor: Maria Spano
Senior Production Editor: Michael Hylton
Senior Production Manager: Greg Steffen
Senior Production Manager, Subsidiary Rights:
Lina s Palma-Temena

ROOTS of PEACE

REPLANTED PAPER

Insight Editions, in association with Roots of Peace, will plant two trees
for each tree used in the manufacturing of this book. Roots of Peace
is an internationally renowned humanitarian organization dedicated
to eradicating land mines worldwide and converting war-torn lands
into productive farms.

Manufactured in China by Insight Editions

10 9 8 7 6 5 4 3 2 1